Date Due

DEC 0 1 2003			

Matthew's Midnight Adventures

Matthew's Midnight Adventures

Matthew and the Midnight Tow Truck
Matthew and the Midnight Turkeys
Matthew and the Midnight Money Van

by Allen Morgan
illustrated by Michael Martchenko

PRINCE OF PEACE LUTHERAN CHURCH & SCHOOL

Annick Press Ltd.
Toronto • New York • Vancouver

For Matthew M.
Matthew and the Midnight Tow Truck

For Robin M.
Matthew and the Midnight Turkeys

For Anna M.
Matthew and the Midnight Money Van

© 2001 Annick Press Ltd.
Cover illustration by Michael Martchenko

Matthew and the Midnight Tow Truck
    ©1984 Allen Morgan (text)
    ©1984 Michael Martchenko (illustrations)
Matthew and the Midnight Turkeys
    ©1985 Allen Morgan (text)
    ©1985 Michael Martchenko (illustrations)
Matthew and the Midnight Money Van
    ©1987 Allen Morgan (text)
    ©1987 Michael Martchenko (illustrations)

We acknowledge the support of the Canada Council for the Arts, the Ontario Arts Council, and the Government of Canada through the Book Publishing Industry Development Program (BPIDP) for our publishing activities.

Cataloging in Publication Data
Morgan, Allen, 1946-
    Matthew and the midnight stories

(Matthew's midnight adventure series)
Contents: Matthew and the midnight money van — Matthew and the midnight tow truck — Matthew and the midnight turkeys.
ISBN 1-55037-699-3

I. Martchenko, Michael. II. Title. III. Series: Morgan, Allen, 1946- .
Matthew's midnight adventure series.

PS8576.O642M293 2001   jC813'.54   C2001-930103-0
PZ7.M8203Maw 2001

The art in this book was rendered in watercolor.
The text was typeset in Korinna.

Distributed in Canada by:
Firefly Books Ltd.
3680 Victoria Park Avenue
Willowdale, ON
M2H 3K1

Published in the U.S.A. by Annick Press (U.S.) Ltd.
Distributed in the U.S.A. by:
Firefly Books (U.S.) Inc.
P.O. Box 1338
Ellicott Station
Buffalo, NY 14205

Printed and bound in Belgium.

visit us at: **www.annickpress.com**

Contents

Matthew and the

Midnight Tow Truck

One night Matthew was playing with his cars in the kitchen while he waited for his supper to cook. First he took his tow truck and hooked onto a station wagon, he towed it right up onto the table top and dropped it off on his plate. Then he drove back down to get another one. Towing all his cars away made Matthew feel hungry so he told his mother that they needed something special for dessert.

"Let's go down to the store and get some red licorice," he said.

"Sorry," said his mother. "You've had enough candy already today. You don't need any more."

Matthew didn't agree at all. He told his mother that he needed red licorice a lot but she just shook her head.

"Not tonight," she said. "Tonight you're having fruit cocktail. Now take those cars off your plate so I can serve supper."

Later that night, just before bedtime when Matthew was counting his cars he discovered that one of his vans was missing. He told his mother right away and they looked all around the bedroom for it. But even though they looked everywhere, they couldn't find Matthew's missing van.

"It's getting late," said his mother finally. "I'm afraid it's time to go to bed. We'll have to find your van some other time."

"But it's my very best one," Matthew told his mother as she tucked him in. "I'll bet it's lost for good now, I'll bet I never see it again."

His mother kissed him goodnight and told him not to worry.

"You can look for it when you wake up," she said as she turned out the light. "It's bound to turn up one way or another."

Matthew hoped that she was right. Even so, when he fell asleep, he was feeling a little sad.

Later that night, just after midnight, Matthew woke up. He saw a flashing red light shining in through his window so he jumped out of bed and went to see what was happening outside.

A big black midnight tow truck was standing in the middle of the street right in front of Matthew's house. The driver was working on one of the cars that was parked at the curb. He was trying to hook onto the bumper, but the hook was too big and it kept slipping off.

The midnight tow truck driver was just about to give up when he looked up and saw Matthew at the window. His face broke into a great big grin then.

"Hey kid!" he shouted up at Matthew. "Come on outside here, will ya? I'm going to need some help hooking this one!"

Matthew went downstairs. He went very quietly because he didn't want to wake up his mother. He put on his boots and his jacket and then he went outside. The midnight tow truck driver was waiting for him. He slapped Matthew on the back.

"Hi kid!" he said. "Glad you could make it. This job is going to take the two of us. Grab the hook, will ya?"

Matthew grabbed the hook and held it on the bumper while the midnight tow truck driver worked the crank. In no time at all the job was done and the car was ready to be towed away.

"Not bad kid, not bad at all," said the midnight tow truck driver. "You do good work. Want to help me hook some more cars?"

"Sure!" said Matthew and he climbed up into the front seat.

Matthew and the midnight tow truck driver went all around the city that night hooking cars together. First they got a station wagon. Then they picked up a van. Matthew was feeling a little hungry from all the work. So was the midnight tow truck driver.

"Let's pull over and have a snack," he suggested.

They stopped at an empty parking lot just beside the railroad tracks. The midnight tow truck driver got out his lunchbox and opened it. The lunchbox was full of red licorice.

"Take some," said the midnight tow truck driver. "Take as much as you need. You can never get enough red licorice you know. It's good for you and it gives you big muscles."

Matthew and the midnight tow truck driver sat and ate red licorice for a while.

"What do you do with all the cars you hook?" asked Matthew.

"I collect them," said the midnight tow truck driver. "I'm trying to get one of every kind, but I pick up doubles sometimes so I can trade with the other guys."

Just then, another tow truck drove into the lot and the man who was driving it called over to them.

"Hey, that's a nice-looking station wagon you got hooked there," he shouted. "What do you want for it?"

"You got any Jeeps?" asked the midnight tow truck driver.

"Sure I got Jeeps," the man answered. "All kinds of them!"

"Well come over to my place tomorrow after lunch," the midnight tow truck driver told him. "We can trade."

"I'll be there," promised the other man and then he drove away.

When the red licorice was all gone, the midnight tow truck driver drove over to a car wash. Matthew helped him unhook the cars they were towing and then they pushed them inside.

The midnight tow truck driver opened a secret door on the wall of the car wash and Matthew saw a special button there.

"What's that for?" he asked.

"That button makes the car wash shrink the cars," said the midnight tow truck driver and he reached in and pushed it.

The car wash started to work. Water splashed and the big brushes began to spin. Special shrinking soap squirted out of some secret nozzles and covered the cars.

Sure enough, when the cars came out the other end they were all shrunk down to pocket size.

The midnight tow truck driver picked them up and dried them off with his handkerchief. He grinned at Matthew.

"Listen kid, I'll tell you what. You helped me hook three cars tonight. So I was wondering, why don't you just keep one for yourself? Take it home with you, what do you think?"

Matthew thought it was a good idea. He took the van and put it into his jacket pocket.

It was almost morning so the midnight tow truck driver drove Matthew home and dropped him off.

"I was thinking," said Matthew. "My mother has a car, it's that one over there. You wouldn't tow it away by mistake some night, would you?"

"Kid, I'd never!" said the midnight tow truck driver.

"What about the other guys?" asked Matthew.

"Good thing you mentioned it," said the midnight tow truck driver. "I'll tell them to lay off too. Just stick a piece of red licorice under the windshield wiper so they'll know it's yours."

Matthew promised that he would all right, he said goodnight and then he went inside. He took off his boots, he hung up his jacket, and then he went upstairs and got into bed. Soon he was fast asleep.

Later that morning around about six, Matthew woke up again. He ran downstairs and checked his jacket. Sure enough, the van was there in his pocket, just the way he remembered it. So Matthew brought his van upstairs to show to his mother.

"Time to get up!" Matthew told her. "Look! I found my van!"

"Your what?" asked his mother and she sat up in bed. "Oh, your van, that's nice," she said and she lay back in bed and tried to go back to sleep.

But Matthew didn't let her. He ran right into the room.

"The van was in my jacket pocket!" he said as he jumped on the bed. "I bet you'll never guess how it got there!"

Matthew was right. His mother couldn't guess so Matthew had to tell her. She was very interested to hear the story.

"You certainly were busy last night," she said.

"We hooked a lot of cars all right," agreed Matthew. "But you don't have to worry about your car. The midnight tow truck driver is going to make sure that nobody gets it."

"Well I'm glad to hear that," said his mother.

"The only thing is, we'll need some red licorice just to make sure," said Matthew and he explained what they had to do.

"I guess we'll have to go down to the store and buy some," said his mother. "It looks like we really need some red licorice after all."

"Yes we do," said Matthew and he gave his mother a great big hug.

Matthew and the

Midnight Turkeys

One morning Matthew woke up before his mother did. He went into her bedroom to see if she wanted to play. She didn't.

"It's not even six yet!" she told him. "Go back to bed."

Matthew went back to his room but he didn't feel like sleeping much. He decided to fall out of bed instead.

"What are you doing in there?" called his mother.

"I'm falling into a hole," Matthew told her.

"Could you do it a little more quietly?" asked his mother.

So Matthew turned around and around until he fell down and he fell into holes that way for a while. It made him so dizzy he had to laugh.

"Be quiet, you turkey!" his mother called down the hall.

"I can't," Matthew called back. "Whenever I get dizzy I tickle myself. I'm hungry. Can I make my own breakfast?"

"I should say not," said his mother. "You're much too silly today."

So Matthew's mother had to get out of bed and make breakfast herself.

Afterwards, Matthew went out into the yard. A dog was digging a hole in the garden, so he chased it away. Then he got his shovel, two buckets and his best bulldozer, so he could finish the job properly. He worked very hard for a long time and when his mother came out to see what he was up to, she was very surprised to see how much he had done.

"Matthew!" she cried. "You've dug a hole in my garden!"

"Yes I have," said Matthew proudly.

"Lucky for you I haven't planted any flowers there yet," said his mother. "Now fill up that hole right away."

"But it's my very best one," said Matthew. "Can't I keep it for a while?"

"Oh, all right," said his mother. "You can dig there today. But tomorrow that hole has to go, okay?"

When Matthew came in for lunch he was very hungry.

"I'll have two peanut butter and banana sandwiches with plenty of honey inside them," he told his mother. "I'm making my hole into a trap and tonight I am going to catch the midnight turkeys."

"The midnight turkeys?" said his mother. "What are they?"

"They're the turkeys that come out just at midnight," said Matthew. "Midnight turkeys are silly you know, very, very silly. They are so silly they will fall right into my trap for sure."

Matthew washed his hands and sat down at the table. After lunch he had to wash them again because of the sandwiches.

When Matthew went outside he decided it might be a good idea to leave some of his things in the trap so the midnight turkeys would have something to do when they fell in. He brought out his comic books and a deck of cards, a couple of cars and his telephone, a few of his better bottle tops and many other things that midnight turkeys are fond of.

Then he made some signs with arrows on them, so the midnight turkeys would know which way to go. A few of the signs had words on them too, just in case the midnight turkeys could read a little.

When everything was ready Matthew called his mother and showed her his midnight turkey trap.

"Very nice," she said. "But what makes you think they will come tonight?"

"Oh, they'll come all right," said Matthew. "Midnight turkeys always come if you put out a trap for them."

"I see," said his mother. "And what are you planning to do with the midnight turkeys once you catch them?"

"I'll have them for breakfast," Matthew explained. "Midnight turkeys make a very good meal you know."

Then Matthew went inside to have his dinner, he took a bath and got into bed. Soon he was fast asleep.

But later that night, just after midnight, Matthew woke up again. He ran to his window and looked out to see if the midnight turkeys were coming. They were.

They were walking right down the middle of the street and they certainly were silly all right. They were tickling each other and giggling together and one of the sillier ones was even tickling himself, which is quite hard to do.

Then the midnight turkeys took off their shoes and threw them away, they pulled off their socks and tied them in knots. They laughed and giggled and wiggled their bums, they pushed out their bellies and bumped each other whenever they could, and when they did they said, "Excuse me," and fell down.

Then all the midnight turkeys stood under a street light together and sang a sentimental song about underwear.

After a while the midnight turkeys noticed the signs that Matthew had made and they got quite excited. The ones that could read them read what they said and the ones that couldn't ate them instead, just in case they tasted like something.

In no time at all the midnight turkeys were following the arrows and they found Matthew's trap, no problem. They all lined up and waited their turn to fall into the hole, and it wasn't very long before every single one of them was caught.

Matthew went outside to see if his trap was working the way it was supposed to. It was. The midnight turkeys had settled right in and they were having a wonderful time.

"Hey you turkeys!" yelled Matthew. "How do you like it?"

"We love it!" they answered. "This is the best trap we've been caught in for years. Come on, come in, there's plenty of room!"

So Matthew jumped down into the hole and all the midnight turkeys tickled him for a while just to make him feel at home.

Matthew laughed so much it made him feel hungry. The midnight turkeys were hungry too, so they phoned out for pizza. The delivery man came by with their order right away.

"Ten super-large jumbos with anything on them!" he called as he dropped the pizzas down into the hole.

"Let's play cards while we eat," said Matthew.

"Let's play crazy-eights!" yelled a midnight turkey.

"Crazy-eights with crazy nines!" shouted another.

"Crazy tens and aces too!" cried a third.

"Why don't we just have crazy everything!" said Matthew.

So all that night they ate pizza and played cards, and when they got tired of that they ate the cards and played with the pizza. Then they sang some turkey songs together until the night was almost over and the sun was coming up.

"Come on inside," said Matthew. "It's time to eat again."

Everyone agreed so Matthew brought the midnight turkeys into the kitchen and had them for breakfast.

The midnight turkeys made the meal.

"We're going to make cereal sandwiches," they said.

The midnight turkeys got out the bread and they spread a lot of jam around.

"The jam is to keep the cereal from falling out," they said and they were absolutely right because when they poured on the cereal, some of it stuck.

"I like bananas on my cereal sometimes," said Matthew.

"No problem," said the midnight turkeys and they rolled some bananas out flat with the rolling pin and stuck them into the sandwich.

Then the midnight turkeys poured some orange juice into a bowl and they added some tomato juice too until the color was right. Next they put in some ginger ale, some grape juice, some cola, and then, just to make sure it was sweet enough, they dumped in a tin of chocolate syrup and stirred it up.

"The juice-of-many-flavors is good for you," they explained. "It is full of vitamins and lots of other stuff."

After a while the midnight turkeys had to go, so Matthew said goodnight. Then he curled up in his chair. Soon he was fast asleep.

Later that morning around about eight, Matthew's mother woke up. It was very quiet and no one was bouncing on her bed.

"Matthew?" she said. "Matthew, where are you?"

Matthew didn't answer so his mother had to get out of bed and go looking for him. When she finally found him asleep in the kitchen, she was very surprised to see that breakfast was ready.

"Good heavens!" she cried. "What happened?"

Matthew woke up. He looked at his mother and smiled.

"The midnight turkeys got caught in my trap just like I thought they would," he told her. "I jumped in too and we had lots of fun so afterwards I had them for breakfast. The midnight turkeys made a very good meal. I saved you some."

Matthew's mother took a long look around. She saw there were lots of left-overs and she noticed a number of left-unders too. Then she sighed and sat down.

"I don't need any breakfast right now," she said. "What I need is a cup of coffee."

Matthew and the
Midnight Money Van

On the night before Mother's Day Matthew went up to his room right after supper and closed his door tight. He didn't want his mother to know what he was doing, so he put up a sign saying,

"Mothers Keep Out"

and then he got under his bed just in case she didn't.

Matthew was making a Mother's Day card, and he wanted it to be a surprise. He worked very hard for a very long time, and when it was done it looked really good. But even so, Matthew wanted to buy his mother a present too.

One of his cars was a money van, and it had a slot at the top so it could be used as a bank. Matthew opened it up, and he dumped out the pennies to see how many there were. He had quite a few, but Matthew knew there weren't quite enough to buy anything decent. He sighed as he dropped the pennies back down inside the money van one by one.

"I wish I were rich," he thought. "If I were rich I could buy my mother something really good and she'd know how I really feel."

When Matthew was hiding his card away he discovered a box of cereal he was keeping in case he got hungry. He wondered if there was a prize inside so he poured out the cereal to see. His mother came in before he found out.

"What are you doing under the bed?" she said.

Matthew didn't want to tell her, so his mother got down on her hands and knees to see for herself. When she saw all the cereal, she asked Matthew why he was keeping it there.

"It's in case I need breakfast in bed," he said.

His mother frowned and she looked down under the bed again. This time she found an apple, some cheese, a piece of toast and most of a banana. She wasn't too pleased, and it wasn't too long before Matthew and his mother were having a talk together about whether or not his bed was a fridge. They decided it wasn't, and Matthew said he'd do his best to put back the rest of his snacks in the morning.

Then it was time for bed. It was raining outside, so Matthew just lay in the dark for a while listening to raindrops. Finally, at last, he fell fast asleep.

Later that night, just before midnight, Matthew woke up. The rain had stopped and the stars were out. The night was quiet and still. A golden glow was shining in through the window, so Matthew got up to see what it was.

The street was covered with pennies. There must have been a million of them, two million maybe or even more, three million, four, five million shiny, bright, sparkling, new pennies.

A midnight money van came down the street, and it stopped right in front of the house. The driver got out, and he began to sweep up the pennies. Matthew ran outside.

"It's been raining money!" he cried.

"You better believe it!" said the midnight money man.

"It sure rained a lot!" said Matthew.

"A regular cloudburst!" agreed the midnight money man. "It's the best bit of weather we've had for years! You want to help sweep? The two of us could really clean up!"

"You mean we can keep the pennies?" asked Matthew.

"Absolutely!" said the midnight money man. "They're all for free. We'll split them up right down the middle: fifty-fifty for you, fifty-fifty for me, who knows, maybe more, sixty-sixty, who cares, there's so many pennies, we'll both be millionaires!"

So Matthew and the midnight money man got right to work. They swept and swept, and after a while they had a big pile of pennies. Then Matthew got up on top of the van and he poured them all in through the slot.

"Let's drive around and get some more," Matthew said. "I'll bet there's some pennies on the other streets too!"

He was right about that, there were pennies just lying around all over the place! So Matthew and the midnight money man drove all around town in the money van, just picking them up.

They weren't the only ones out there either. The midnight mounted geese police were cleaning the pennies up off the streets with bamboni machines. Many of the midnight turkeys were there. They were flipping the pennies up into the air yelling, "Heads or tails!" at the top of their lungs, and some of the sillier ones even flipped themselves to see which way they'd land. The mysterious moose was out there too, and the dangerous pigeons were hanging around just lurking for trouble.

When the van was all full to the top of the slot, the midnight money man checked the meter to see if they'd got as much as they thought. They had. They had more. The meter said four million dollars!

Matthew and the midnight money man were both very hungry so they went back to Matthew's house for a midnight snack. They had cornflakes and cola. Matthew knew it was not too nutritious, but cornflakes and cola were the midnight money man's very best favorite, so what could Matthew do?

"My mother *always* says that the guest's *always* right, and I *always* do just what my mother says," Matthew explained.

"Good for you!" said the midnight money man. "I'm the same way myself, whenever I can. There's no other person quite like a mother; take mine, she's one of a kind."

Then he took out his wallet and he showed a few photos, so Matthew could see how she looked.

"She looks very nice, you must like her a lot," Matthew told him.

"We go back a long way," agreed the midnight money man.

"I've known my mother a long time too," said Matthew. "That's her on the fridge. I drew her myself. She's the very best mother that ever there was, and now that I'm rich I'm going to get her the very best present there is!"

"Holy Goalies!" said the midnight money man. "It's Mother's Day. I completely forgot! I've got to get something for my mother too. Let's go to the Mall, they're having a sale."

So Matthew and the midnight money man got into the van, and they drove to the Mall right away.

MIDNIGHT MADNESS AT THE MIDNIGHT MALL said a sign on the door. It was definitely true. The midnight turkeys were rolling around all over the Mall doing skatey-eight kilos an hour on their skateboards.

"It's madness!" they screamed, then they threw all their cash up into the air and crashed into whichever wall seemed convenient.

"Are the turkeys here for the sale too?" asked Matthew.

"Sure," said the midnight money man. "We've all got a mother of some kind or other, even the turkeys."

He was right about that. Everyone there had a mother somewhere and they all wanted to get her something decent. The midnight mounted geese police bought suitcases with wheels underneath, so their mothers could ride around airports. The dangerous pigeons bought spraybomb perfume. The mysterious moose bought a big box of candy, and he signed the card, "To my mom from guess who?" The midnight turkeys went straight to the joke store, and they bought up every dribble glass and whoopie cushion in sight.

The midnight money man got an electric fan to keep his mother cool.

"She gets hot in July," he explained to Matthew, and he decided to buy an electric blanket too, just in case she wanted to get hot again in January.

It didn't take Matthew long to find what he was looking for. There was a shiny-new, solid-gold, real-diamond ring in the window of a jewelry store. Matthew knew it was just the sort of thing his mother really liked, so he went inside and asked how much. The ring cost a couple of million.

"That'll clean you right out," said the midnight money man. "Two million's too much for a Mother's Day gift."

"No it's not," Matthew told him. "My mother's the very best mother I know, so I might as well buy her the best."

It was getting quite late, so the midnight money man drove Matthew home, and he said goodbye.

"If you ever get rich again someday, just give me a shout and I'll help you out!" he called as he drove away.

"Okay," called back Matthew. "I will."

He went inside and he put the shiny-new, solid-gold, real-diamond ring away in a very secret place so it wouldn't get lost. Then he got into bed. Soon he was fast asleep.

Later that morning, around about five, Matthew woke up. He knew right away what day it was, and he remembered all about the secret surprise he had bought for his mother.

"I hope it's still safe," he thought.

It certainly was. It was very safe. In fact it was so completely safe that Matthew couldn't even find it. He tried very hard to remember just where he'd put it the night before. He looked all around for an hour or more in all his most secret places, but even so, the shiny-new, solid-gold, real-diamond ring just couldn't be found.

Around about six he had to give up. It was getting quite late and Matthew knew he wouldn't be able to give his mother such a big surprise if he waited much longer.

"My present has to be the very first thing she sees when she opens her eyes," he said. "I'll have to think of some other thing I can give to my mother instead of a ring."

Matthew decided that breakfast in bed could be quite surprising if done the right way. He went to his room and crawled under the bed. He put all the food he was saving there on a breakfast tray, and he carried it in to his mother.

"Surprise!" he cried. "Happy Mother's Day!"

"Happy what?" asked his mother, and she opened one eye. "Happy who?"

So Matthew sang "Happy Mother's Day To You," until she could open her other eye too. Then he showed his mother the card he had made and he gave her some breakfast.

His mother was certainly very surprised. So was Matthew. When he poured out the cereal the shiny-new, solid-gold, real-diamond ring rolled out of the box and into the bowl.

"Holy Granola!" cried Matthew. "So that's where it was! I knew it was somewhere!"

His mother didn't understand, so Matthew had to tell her all about the midnight money van and how it had been raining pennies that night.

"I bought you the ring at the Midnight Mall," he explained. "It was the very best one, so I got it for you. You're the very best mother that ever was, too!"

"And you're the very best boy," said his mother. She gave him a hug. "You should have bought something for yourself too!"

"That's okay," Matthew told her. "It's sure to rain pennies again, you'll see, and then, when it does, we'll go shopping for me!"

Books by Allen Morgan, published by Annick Press:

Matthew and the Midnight Tow Truck
Matthew and the Midnight Turkeys
Matthew and the Midnight Money Van
Nicole's Boat

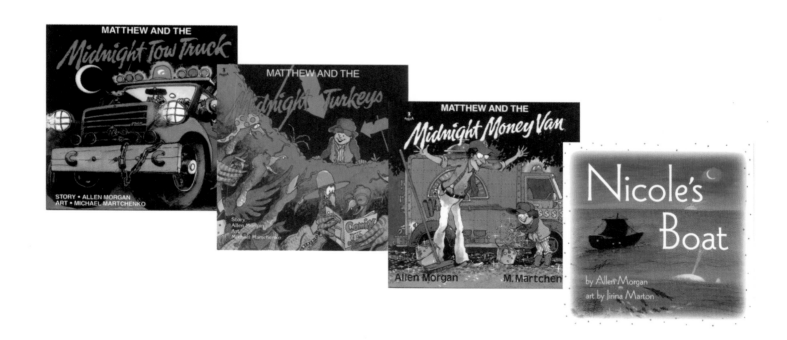